P9-DCD-914

They walked in line across the meadow, through their own dead from the day before. Charley tried not to look down at them but couldn't help it and found that they all looked alike. He could not identify men he'd known for months. They were all bloated, pushing out against their uniforms; clouds of flies were planting eggs in the wound openings and eyes and mouths of the bodies. The smell was sweet, cloying, the smell of blood and dirt and decaying flesh—the smell of death. They had uniforms on, red flannel shirts, so he knew they were all Minnesota men, but the dead all looked alike.

Broken. Like broken toys or dolls.

ALSO BY GARY PAULSEN

GARY PAULSEN

SOLDIER'S HEART

**BEING THE STORY
OF THE ENLISTMENT
AND DUE SERVICE
OF THE BOY CHARLEY GODDARD
IN THE FIRST MINNESOTA VOLUNTEERS**

A Novel of the Civil War

Published by
Dell Laurel-Leaf
an imprint of Random House Children's Books
a division of Random House, Inc.
1540 Broadway
New York, New York 10036

If you purchased this book without a cover you should be aware that this book is stolen property. It was reported as "unsold and destroyed" to the publisher and neither the author nor the publisher has received any payment for this "stripped book."

Copyright © 1998 by Gary Paulsen

All rights reserved. No part of this book may be reproduced or transmitted in any form or by any means, electronic or mechanical, including photocopying, recording, or by any information storage and retrieval system, without the written permission of the Publisher, except where permitted by law. For information address Delacorte Press, 1540 Broadway, New York, New York 10036.

The trademark Laurel-Leaf Library® is registered in the U.S. Patent and Trademark Office.
The trademark Dell® is registered in the U.S. Patent and Trademark Office.

Visit us on the Web! www.randomhouse.com/teens

Educators and librarians, for a variety of teaching tools, visit us at
www.randomhouse.com/teachers

ISBN 0-440-22838-7

RL: 5.9

Reprinted by arrangement with Delacorte Press

Printed in the United States of America

September 2000

40 39 38 37 36 35 34 33 32 31

OPM

*Dedicated to
Mike Magee—
friend, sailor and
one who understands . . .*

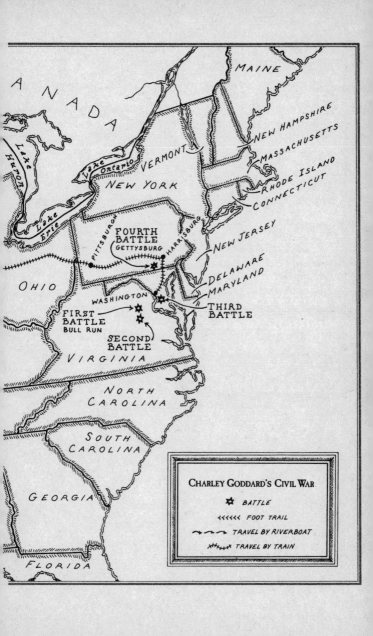

CONTENTS

War is always, in all ways, appalling. Lives are stopped in youth, worlds are ended, and even for those who survive—and the vast majority of soldiers who go to war *do* survive—the mental damage done is often permanent. What they have seen and been forced to do is frequently so horrific and devastating that it simply cannot be tolerated by the human psyche.

Now there is an attempt to understand this form of injury and deal with it. It is called posttraumatic stress disorder by those who try to cure it. They give it a technical name in the attempt to make something almost incomprehensible understandable, in the hope that, by doing this, they will make it curable.

But in other times and other wars, they used more descriptive terms.

In the Second World War the mental damage was called battle fatigue, and there were rudimentary efforts to help the victims. These usually involved bed rest and the use of sedatives or other drugs.

In the First World War it was called shell shock, based on the damage done by the overwhelming use, for the first time in modern war, of artillery fire against soldiers in stationary positions (trenches). The concussion of exploding incoming rounds, thousands upon thousands of them, often left men deaf and dazed, many of them with a symptom called the thousand-yard stare. The afflicted were essentially not helped at all and simply sent home for their families to care for. Most were irrational; many were in a vegetative state.

In the Civil War the syndrome was generally not recognized at all. While the same horrors existed as those in modern war, in some ways they were even worse because the technological aspect of war being born then, the whole-sale killing by men using raw firepower, was so new and misunderstood. The same young men were fed into the madness. But in those days there was no scientific knowledge of mental disorders and no effort was made to help the men who were damaged. Some men came through combat unscathed. Most did not. These men were somehow different from other men.

They were said to have soldier's heart.

SOLDIER'S HEART

CHAPTER ONE

❖—◆—❖

JUNE 1861

He heard it all, Charley did; heard the drums and songs and slogans and knew what everybody and his rooster was crowing.

There was going to be a shooting war. They were having town meetings and nailing up posters all over Minnesota and the excitement was so high Charley had seen girls faint at the meetings, just faint from the noise and hullabaloo. It was better than a circus. Or what he thought a circus must be like. He'd never seen one. He'd never seen anything but Winona,

Minnesota, and the river five miles each way from town.

There would be a shooting war. There were rebels who had violated the law and fired on Fort Sumter and the only thing they'd respect was steel, it was said, and he knew they were right, and the Union was right, and one other thing they said as well—if a man didn't hurry he'd miss it. The only shooting war to come in a man's life and if a man didn't step right along he'd miss the whole thing.

Charley didn't figure to miss it. The only problem was that Charley wasn't rightly a man yet, at least not to the army. He was fifteen and while he worked as a man worked, in the fields all of a day and into night, and looked like a man standing tall and just a bit thin with hands so big they covered a stove lid, he didn't make a beard yet and his voice had only just dropped enough so he could talk with men.

If they knew, he thought, if they knew he was but fifteen they wouldn't take him at all.

But Charley watched and Charley listened and Charley learned.

Minnesota was forming a volunteer regiment to go off and fight. It would have near on a thousand men when it was full, men from Winona and Taylor's Falls and Mankato and as far north as Deerwood and from the capital, St. Paul, as well.

A thousand men. And Charley had learned one thing about an army: One part of an army didn't always know the business of another part. The thousand men in the regiment would be in companies of eighty to a hundred men from each section and it would be hard for a man to know men who weren't from the same area.

Charley couldn't join where they knew him. Somebody would spill the beans and he'd get sent back or used as a runner or drummer boy. He wasn't any boy. He was going to sign to fight as a man and he knew a way to do it.

They would gather at Fort Snelling, up along

the Mississippi. All the companies from all the towns would assemble there before they went off to fight.

He'd just take him a walk, Charley would, take a walk by himself until he was at Fort Snelling and there he would lie about his age and sign up as a man and get him a musket and a uniform and go to see what a war was like.

"I won't get into any trouble, Ma," he said, wrapping some bread and cold potatoes and half a roast chicken in some tow cotton. "Plus they'll be paying me. I hear they give eleven dollars a month. I'll send most of it on home to you and Orren." Orren was his younger brother. "You can use the money and I won't be under your feet all the time. . . ."

"You aren't under my feet." She hated it when he talked fast. He always got his way when he talked fast. He'd smile and that cowlick would stand up in the back and he'd talk fast and she couldn't keep him from what he wanted. He was a good boy, as good as they came, but ever since his father, Paul, had been kicked to death by a horse gone mad when a swarm of bees landed on it, Charley only had to smile and talk fast and he got his way. "You haven't ever been under my feet."

"Same as," he said, shaking his head. "I'm always in the way. Best I go off and see what the big fuss is all about."

"You ain't but a boy."

"And I've got to be a man sometime. You've said it more than once yourself. Charley, you said, you've got to be a man. Well, here it is— my chance to be a man. A boy wouldn't go off to earn eleven dollars a month and wear a uniform. Only a man. So I'm going to be a man and do what a man can do."

And he won. She knew he would and he did and he took his bread and cold potatoes and chicken and left home walking down the road for Fort Snelling, and if she had known what was to come of it, if she had known and could tell him what would come of it, she would have fought to drag him back and let the federal government keep their eleven dollars a month.

But she also had heard the songs and the slogans and seen the parades, had been to the meetings, and though it was her son Charley leaving she did not think it would be so bad. Nobody thought it would be so bad. Nobody thought it *could* be so bad. And all the officers and politicians and newspapers said it would be a month or two, no longer.

It would all be over by fall.

CHAPTER TWO

FORT SNELLING

They didn't have uniforms for him. There was a pair of black pants that were so short his calves showed, a pair of gray socks and a black felt hat. That was the uniform he received to go for a soldier. The socks and pants were stout but the hat was cheap and with the first little sprinkle it sagged around his head and drooped over his face.

They took his name. The colonel of the regiment read a list of things he couldn't do—desert his post, traffic with the enemy, steal from his fellow soldiers, act immoral or without decency—and then he signed his name, told them he was eighteen and they didn't challenge it, and he was a soldier. He could read and write, Charley could, though he hadn't had much schooling. His ma had made him stick to reading and writing and he wrote her letters telling her of how it was to be a soldier.

"The food is bad," he wrote. "Beef so gamey dogs won't eat it, and hard beans. We bile the beans and use them for a meal, then use the leftover beans for soup the next day and on the third day take any cooked beans that are left, dry them and crush them and boil them for coffee. The men don't like them much and there's talk of hanging the commissary officer. It ain't but just talk, but some don't smile when they say it."

There wasn't much of a war, Charley decided early on, but there was a lot of playacting and once he got inside it he found it mostly boring.

They did something they called "drills" and

the "manual of arms," working in the hot sun in the compound area of Fort Snelling until they were soaked with sweat and Charley felt he could snap his rifle from left shoulder heft to right shoulder heft as good as any man in any army had ever done it.

They fired some but there wasn't much ammunition and when the sergeants tried to make them hit targets a quarter mile off, Charley nearly laughed. He'd hunted his whole life and knew about shooting, but the rifles they were issued were .58-caliber rifled muskets that fired a hollow-base bullet called a minié ball, named after the Frenchman who had invented it. The rifles thundered but lacked the flat crack of his smaller-bore hunting rifle, and he found that nearly a third of the time the bullet seemed to fly end over end and it was all he could do to hit a target fifty yards off. A quarter mile— over four hundred yards—seemed silly.

But they practiced anyway and stood and fired and dropped to one knee, and then the next rank stood and fired and dropped. They reloaded by biting the end off the paper cartridge, pouring the powder down the bore and setting the bullet on the powder with the ramrod. Then a cap on the nipple, the hammer back and fire again—they said a man could do it three times a minute but Charley somehow never managed more than twice.

When they couldn't afford to expend any more live ammunition they practiced with empty rifles, again and again, until Charley was sick to death of the drilling and wheeling and marching and fake loading.

It would be different, he thought, if the leaders knew what they were doing. But the officers and sergeants had been civilians like the rest of the men and mostly had been elected by the men themselves and had to learn as they went along, using an army manual for close-order drill.

It seemed all they did was drill and sweat and listen to sergeants and corporals bellow at them and as the weeks passed Charley grew more and more bored and was beginning to pay attention to his mother's letters. She had taken to thinking of the bad side of the war and was in fear that Charley would get killed and wrote three times a week.

"I know it ain't right," she wrote in one letter, "but you must think on coming home now. Just leave the army and walk home before they get you in a battle and shoot you apart. . . ."

Like most of the men, Charley doubted there ever would be a battle. Minnesota was mostly wild then, with Sioux and Chippewa Indians to the north and west, and there were some frontier forts on the edge of the wilderness to deal with any difficulties. These posts were manned by regular army troops, which Lincoln needed now to fight in the war, and there was talk in the ranks that the Minnesota volunteers would be used to replace the army troops at the frontier forts so the regular army could go east to fight.

"It'll be all mosquitoes and muck," a corporal named Massey said during a break in drilling one afternoon. "They don't let me go fight the rebels and I might pull foot and leave. . . ."

It was all rumor, of course, but what with his mother's letters (she wrote more often all the time of deserting), the boredom of constant drilling in the hot sun, and now the talk of being sent to relieve the frontier forts so that the regular army troops could go fight the Rebels (one company had already been started on the march north to the forts), Charley was nearly on the edge of leaving when on June 22 they were called into formation, ordered to get all their gear and marched to the river, where steamboats were waiting to take them to St. Paul.

There they marched through town with great fanfare. They still didn't have proper uniforms but they had all been issued red flannel shirts, and though those shirts were as hot as original sin—as Charley heard them described—at least the men looked like a unit, marching with shouldered rifles and hats cocked forward. Girls waved flags and people yelled, "Go it, boys, get the Rebels!" and "Don't stop till you hit Richmond!"

In a short time they boarded other steamboats that took them south and east to La Crosse, Wisconsin, where trains were waiting for them.

It was all new to him. Charley had never ridden on a steamboat, never marched in a parade or had pretty girls wave flags for him and hand him sweets. Now, as he boarded the train and saw the plush seats and fancy inside of the car, he thought: I never, I just never imagined such a thing existed.

It was, all in all, a simply grand way to go off to fight a war.

CHAPTER THREE

TOWARD MANASSAS

He thought he would remember the train ride forever. Most of the men had never been on a train and certainly few of them had been on one this plush. The seats were soft and cushiony and the food—especially compared to the rough fare at Fort Snelling—was delicious.

They rode across Wisconsin and down into Chicago and everywhere they stopped there were huge crowds gathered to cheer them on. Girls gave them hankies and sweets and Charley figured later he had fallen in love at least a dozen times.

The country didn't change much at first and it was still all Union. They made their way—sleeping like lords and eating like kings, Charley thought—across Illinois, Indiana, Ohio, Pennsylvania and down into Maryland, and there were crowds all the way, even when the train didn't stop.

Charley saw his first coloreds when they moved into Maryland. They looked poor and had poor clothes and he thought about slavery then and how it must be strange to own a person so they had to do what you wanted. He'd never considered it before and wondered what would happen after the war when the Union had whipped the Rebels. Would they be allowed to keep their slaves? The war wasn't initially about slavery; the troops were going to stop the "lawbreakers and wrong thinkers" that were trying to "bust up the Union." They talked about it at night while the train moved east and south, and never did they speak of slavery. Just about the wrongheadedness of the Southern "crackers" and how they had to teach Johnny Reb a lesson.

A woman of color came up to him when the train was stopped in Maryland, just before Baltimore, and handed him a sweet roll and said, "Thank you for what you're doing. I hope God keeps you safe from harm and brings you back to your family."

She was crying. Charley thanked her and ate the cake and smiled at her and wondered why she was crying and wanted to ask why she was glad he was going to fight the South—she was, after all, part of the South—but they had to reboard the train then and he never found out why the colored woman was crying. He did see as the train moved off that a white woman came out of the house and grabbed the colored woman by her dress and dragged her back inside. Then she turned and shook her fist at the train.

She's a Reb, he thought, and it surprised him, though he didn't know why he should be surprised that a woman who owned another person would be a Reb. They were in Maryland and had been warned to watch out for Rebels and their sympathizers, but it was still his first experience with a Southerner. He watched the house from the open window as the train pulled away, hoping for another sight of the woman.

Now the country was changing. There had been farms all along, and towns, but the trees seemed more spaced here, the pastures more open, and Charley began to see "poor" farms. He'd heard the men talking about them, the poor whites, but he still wasn't quite ready for the sight when the train slowed for a hill and passed a shack that was little more than boards tacked to some poles. The children running around out front were only half clothed and a man and a woman were sitting in rags. All the soldiers talked about the poor white trash and how these were the people they had come to fight, people who couldn't get out of their yards, let alone fight a proper army.

It made him very conscious of his own home. Even without a father there, the house was in good shape and kept up and there was a well-tended garden, good food, clothes that covered bodies. He wondered how the Rebels thought they could fight a war when their people couldn't dress themselves. It made him sad to see the children barely clothed. What would happen to them in winter? They did not have much of a winter here, he knew—nothing like Minnesota's—but it would still be cold. He turned from the window just as a man next to him, a private named Swenson, said, "You could throw a cat through their house without hitting a wall."

"They don't have anything," Charley said. "Not a thing."

The man nodded.

"This ain't going to be much of a war. I don't see how they can fight. They don't have any clothes."

"Hell, it'll probably be over before we get to Washington," Swenson said, and Charley nodded but stopped talking because he did not like profanity, even of a low order, and there was much of it around. He thought of a surgeon who had spoken to them and told them to try to wear clean clothing going into battle in case they were hit by a rifle ball. If the cloth was carried into the wound, clean cloth would cause less infection. He had thought of it and taken a bullet from one of the paper cartridges and pushed it against his sleeve. It didn't seem possible that the bullet could be made to go through the sleeve, into him, *into* him, carrying the fabric with it.

He thought it must be the same with profanity and immoral thinking. Charley believed in Heaven and Hell and God and Jesus and wanted to be with God if he was killed. If he had profane thoughts as he went to war, they might infect his soul as the dirty clothes would infect his wound. And while he did not think he would die, did not think he would even be hit or hurt, did not think of it at all, still it was best to be careful.

He stared out the window and thought of all the things he would tell his mother and his brother, Orren, when he wrote the next letter.

I'm a man now, he would write, *and seeing and doing a man's things out in the world. I've seen things you wouldn't believe. . . .*

He leaned back, closed his eyes and let the gentle rocking of the train take him to sleep.

CHAPTER FOUR

BULL RUN

Make it stop now! Charley thought, or thought he was thinking until he realized he was screaming it: *"Make it all stop now!"*

Death was everywhere, nowhere. Bullets flew past him with evil little snaps and snickers as they cut the air. Next to him Massey's head suddenly left his body and disappeared, taken by a cannon round that then went through an officer's horse, end to end, before plowing into the ground.

This can't be, he thought. I can't be here. This is all a mistake. A terrible mistake. I'm not supposed to be here.

He had forgotten to fire. The officers had marched them out into a field in perfect order and told them where to aim and fire, and he had raised his rifle and then the whole world had come at him. The Rebel soldiers were up a shallow grade a hundred yards away, behind some fallen trees, and they had opened on Charley and the others before anyone could fire.

It was like a blade cutting grain. He heard the bullets hitting the men—little *thunk-slaps*—and saw the men falling. Some of them screamed as they fell. Most were silent. Many were dead before they hit the ground. Many were torn apart, hit ten or twelve or more times before they had time to drop.

The men left standing with Charley fired, then the survivors of that round reloaded and fired again, and Charley aimed in the general direction of the Rebels and pulled his trigger, firing blind.

The black powder smoke clouded from the rifles and the rebel guns on the hill and it was impossible to see or to understand anything.

I don't know anything, Charley thought—the words jerked through his mind before he thought them.

Somebody screamed over the sound of the gunfire, and the man next to Charley turned to the rear and began walking away as calm as if he was going for a stroll in a park, his rifle at right shoulder heft.

Charley followed him, dragging his own rifle along the ground. He must know something I don't know, he thought—must have heard something—but the man hadn't gone four steps before he was struck in the back several times and dropped on his face.

Bullets filled the air. Charley heard them going past his ears like horizontal hail and he decided to lie down. If he didn't lie down he would be hit, ripped, torn to pieces.

It was only slightly better on the ground. He heard the same sounds, the same bullets, but the bodies in front of him protected him. He could hear bullets hitting them.

Two bullets met directly in front of his eyes, jammed together and fell to the ground, as one. That sight was more horrifying than the death he'd seen. How many bullets, he thought, would have to be flying around for two of them to collide in midair?

Something jerked at his foot, pulling it sideways. He was sure he'd been hit, didn't see how it was possible to *keep* from being hit, but when he turned he saw Lieutenant Olafson tugging at his leg. The officer had been hit in his left upper arm. He was still holding a saber in his left hand and was jerking at Charley with his right.

"Get up, boy. We're to fall back." The cords in his neck bulged with the strain of screaming over the noise.

"Back?"

"In good order we're to fall back to the trees. Come on, son, up now and move. Help some of the others."

Somehow Charley's arms worked to push him off the ground. He stood and started walking when everything in him wanted to run; started walking "in good order" even when the lieutenant was hit in the chest and head and went down, obviously finished, but with legs still moving, still pumping, still pushing the dying body around and around on the ground; Charley started walking, not running, even when his mind prayed to God, told God, demanded of God:

I am not supposed to see this, God. No person is supposed to see this. How can You let this happen?

Charley walked amid the explosions of shot and the ripping of bullets until he was clear of the smoke and saw other men walking with him. Impossible, he thought, that they could walk as they did, in rank; impossible that they had lived, could have lived through what had come at them, was still coming at them.

Many of the men crouched as they moved, as if in a heavy rain, and Charley found himself doing the same, and when he was still some twenty yards from the line of trees ahead he crouched more and then ran—could not stop himself from running—until he was there, in the trees, a large maple at his back, and finally, sucking air until his lungs seemed to be on fire, finally he stopped and leaned over, his hands on his knees, and vomited, heaving until he was empty and then heaving more, until he felt as if his stomach would come up, until he felt his very soul would leave him.

CHAPTER FIVE

NIGHT

Officers moved among the men and told them what every man knew was a lie; told them they'd done well, had stood up to Rebel fire and given it back. But even Charley knew—and he thought he knew nothing—that they'd been whipped from the field. They'd been ordered to cross a meadow and take the hill and the Confederates had torn them to pieces, made them withdraw "in good order," made them run.

But the officers moved through the trees

and told them lies and said to rest because they would have to go back tomorrow, would regroup and move against the Rebels in the morning, and Charley thought it was like trying to tell water to run uphill. There was nothing on God's earth that would allow his legs to move his body against that fire again. Not a man, he thought, not a man would be alive halfway across that meadow.

He lay by a tree and watched fireflies move over the battlefield. They were pretty, flitting here and there, and for a moment he could believe that none of it had happened. The firing was done now, the only sound the moaning of the wounded. The Rebs were back in their woods, resting, just as Charley was, and the pretty fireflies were fluttering around the field over the dead. Then Charley realized they weren't fireflies but lanterns.

They were lanterns and candles. Men from both sides were going from body to body in the dark, looking for dead friends, for wounded comrades, and he thought of men he knew who were out there—Massey, and the lieutenant—but decided it would serve no purpose to go out there and see it all again.

They were dead. He'd seen them die. Massey didn't have a head and the lieutenant didn't have a brain or heart or much of anything else, and short of digging a hole and burying them he didn't know what he could do for them.

Or for me, he thought. I don't know what I can do for me. He watched the lanterns and candles and tried to feel sad for the dead and wounded, tried to feel some pain for them, but he could feel nothing but a bone tiredness that left his hands shaking and his legs weak and his stomach churning.

"Drink water," someone whispered in the darkness; it sounded like another officer's voice. "You all must drink water if you can hold it down. Try to get some sleep. Men will pass among you with rations."

Somebody came out of the dark and handed him a piece of half-dried bread and cold, raw salt pork. He nearly threw the food away but took a small bite of the bread and was immediately ravenously hungry. He wolfed down the bread and ate the raw pork, surprised that it stayed in his stomach. He drank water until his stomach was full and his canteen empty, then let his back slide down the tree until he was sitting with legs outstretched. His head nodded and bobbed and he dozed, fought sleep, then dropped off again until his chin rested on his chest and he was sleeping.

"Check your weapon." Somebody was shaking him and he opened his eyes and felt as stiff as an old man. It seemed just moments had passed but he raised his head and saw a faint grayness in the east. "Clean your weapon and check your load. Refill your cartridge boxes and get more caps. Fill your canteen from the stream back twenty yards and get ready. We move with good light."

Charley stood and walked to a small creek. It took only moments to hold his canteen beneath the surface and let it fill and take several long drinks from the brook and wash his face, but in that time the light grew brighter and he saw that the water wasn't clear, it was tinged with pink, and he saw bodies in the water upstream.

This time he wanted to vomit but it would not come. The food felt like a stone in his stomach and the bloodied water seemed to sour it, curdle it, but it wouldn't come up even when he stuck his finger down his throat.

"Clean your weapon, Private." A sergeant from another part of the regiment, one he did not know, came up to him and pointed to his rifle. "There'll be plenty of time for puking later. Get ready. We're going against them again in just a few minutes."

Later he would know things about fighting. It was silent now and that meant that troops had not joined battle yet; meant that there might not be a fight. But he did not know this yet and the sergeant's order made him so afraid it was as if a shaft had gone through him, had stopped his heart. He had never really thought they would make him cross the meadow again.

But here it was, against him. He looked to where they had been yesterday and saw the lumps that were bodies. Here and there a wounded man—lying all night on the ground— moved and made a small sound but mostly they were still.

I'll be there soon, he thought. I'll be there on the ground with them. If I don't run away I'll be there like a broken doll. We all will. None of us can live if we walk out there again.

But he could not run away. None of the others had and he couldn't. He cleaned his rifle carefully. He had not loaded it after firing the previous afternoon and he used a bit of rag and water to clean out the powder residue, then took oil from a small bottle he carried and oiled the bore and wiped it dry with a piece of rag he carried wrapped around the bottle—all done automatically, without thinking.

The training must work, he thought. I'm doing all this without meaning to do it. He felt like a stranger to himself, like another person watching his hands move over the rifle, wiping and cleaning. When it was clean he snapped three caps on the nipple to burn any oil out of the nipple hole, then took a cartridge from his cartridge box, bit the end of the paper off, poured the powder down the bore, slid the bullet down on top of it and pushed it into place with the ramrod.

When the bullet was seated he cocked the hammer, pinched a cap so it would stay wedged on the nipple and eased the hammer down to half cock.

Ready.

For a moment there was nothing to do, so he started to sit by the tree again, but then the sergeants came.

"Everybody form line-of-battle. Out here, form on me!"

And Charley's legs moved again, carried him out, and he hated them for it but they worked and took him into the grass to stand with all the other men who still lived.

"Form on me, in a line, line-of-battle right here."

A sergeant he did not know was pointing with an officer's saber to where they should stand. The men moved as told, stood in their line, and Charley stood with them.

"Fix bayonets!"

Charley pulled the bayonet from the scabbard at his side and locked it on the muzzle of his rifle.

Another delay. It was a clear morning, no clouds, the sun just up, and he could see other units forming. How could they? he thought. How could they just form and stand there waiting for it after yesterday? How could I? It had all started this way yesterday. March out and form up. Except that yesterday there were congressmen and their families on the hills, come out from Washington in buggies to picnic and watch the battle, and hadn't *they* got more than they bargained for? All those petticoats flying and the carriages rocking along as they found that Rebel shells did not care if you were a soldier or a civilian.

The Union troops had marched the same as today and formed into the same line-of-battle and then the Rebs had brought the fire and steel of God down on them . . .

"Forward!"

The sergeant turned and started marching across the field, just as he had done yesterday, heading for the piles of dead men they'd left yesterday, walking in a measured pace, and the men followed, their rifles held at port arms, ready to be raised.

"Watch the trees," the sergeant yelled. "Keep your eyes on the trees. . . ."

That, Charley thought, was the most unnecessary command he had ever heard. Charley couldn't keep his eyes *off* the trees. His mind, his breath, his very being watched the trees. The trees where his death would come from.

They walked in line across the meadow, through their own dead from the day before. Charley tried not to look down at them but couldn't help it and found that they all looked alike. He could not identify men he'd known for months. They were all bloated, pushing out against their uniforms; clouds of flies were planting eggs in the wound openings and eyes and mouths of the bodies. The smell was sweet, cloying, the smell of blood and dirt and decaying flesh—the smell of death. They had uniforms on, red flannel shirts, so he knew they were all Minnesota men, but the dead all looked alike.

Broken. Like broken toys or dolls.

The troops were through the dead now, still walking, past the smell.

There. He thought he saw movement in the trees. A hundred yards, now ninety-nine, ninety-eight. Every step a yard. Another step, another, men stepping next to him.

There. Some rustling leaves. He was sure of it. Movement. They'd open fire soon. Any second. It would come from the trees. The snarl and smoke and death would come from the trees, from the leaves.

Any second. Now. Now. *Now!* Why don't they shoot? What are they waiting for? Every breath his last, every sound his last, every sight his last—it would come *now*. God oh God oh God *now*!

It did not come.

They walked in line to the Rebel earthworks and found the enemy gone. The Rebs had pulled out during the night. Left food on the fires, water in pails—just left it all.

Charley studied the earthworks. Logs stacked up with dirt piled in front and small ledges for the men to stand on and shoot without exposing more than their heads. We could have shot at them for years and never hit them, Charley thought; we could have died shooting at them and never touched them.

He took a deep breath and let it out—his first whole breath since they had started walking across the meadow—and looked down and was shocked to see that he'd wet himself.

Across the meadow, he thought; I must have done it then. Walking through the bodies.

Maybe then. He couldn't remember doing it, could only remember the fear—it stopped his breath, made him almost *want* to die—and it must have been then.

He started to hide himself, turn away, but he saw that he was not alone, that several other men had done the same thing.

First battle.

CHAPTER SIX

FARMING

The fight had been called the Battle for Manassas Junction by some newspapers Charley saw but it quickly was called Bull Run by the men, for the creek that ran nearby.

They withdrew and set up camp in Washington, where all they did was drill and stand guard duty and wait for the Rebs to come and take the city—which most everybody said they could do with a good company of men—and Charley went to see some sights, but it rained most of the time so he went back to the camp before his pass expired.

The Rebs did not come, and replacements poured into all the units. They were issued new uniforms—heavy wool, proper blue, with black leather belting—and, more important, they were finally paid after nearly three months.

Charley was given thirty-three dollars in gold coins. It was more money than he'd ever had, more money than he'd ever seen, and he was sorely tempted to spend it all on himself. He did not think he would live much longer— not past another battle—and he thought of all the things he could get with the money.

The sutler had come and there were pies for the outrageous sum of twenty-five cents each and he'd been on salt pork and beans for over a month. The thought of a pie was too much and he spent the money for one of them—an apple pie—and sat in his tent alone and ate the whole thing with his fingers, licking the juice from the pan until it was clean. He instantly wanted another.

This he bought, which he also ate alone, and with that his stomach was full at last and the desire to spend money was gone with the fullness. He kept four dollars for possible expenses and sent the rest home by registered mail with a letter to his mother:

"Here is some money. I've been in a battle. I was scart some but it's past now. I can't come home."

And now he waited. They all waited. They drilled and cleaned and cleaned and drilled and were given a new army commander named McClellan that many of the men, Charley included, held in high regard because he sat a horse well and took care to mind the conditions of his soldiers.

In a little time they marched again and some said it was to be a battle but now they had been waiting for so long that many of them did not think there would be a battle at all. They thought they would just keep waiting and waiting and never fight again. It was, of course, a dream, a hope, and for many of them, a prayer.

Charley was not among them. He had waited with them, of course, and had settled into camp life and even marching life, but he still believed in the inevitability of battle and most of all believed in the absolute certainty of his own death. He could not live. Many others would die with him and many would live but he knew one thing:

He would die. In the next battle or the one after that or the one after that he would die.

But for the moment he kept his equipment clean and in good order and as they marched south he found time to look at the country.

There were settled farms now, more prosperous looking than the ones he'd seen from the train. There were chickens and cattle and pigs and barely ripe fruit in the trees. The Minnesota regiment already had a reputation. They were called "cool under fire" and "well disciplined" but although they had been ordered not to forage—steal food from the population as they marched—most men ignored the order. After all, they were passing through Rebel territory and if they left the food the "dirty seceshes" (for "secessionists") would just eat it.

The men called it farming. Charley "farmed" several chickens and helped slaughter a pig and a cow and agreed with the men that "secesh liberation meat" tasted as good as any homegrown goods.

They ate fruit constantly, picked largely green from the trees, and most of the men had bowel troubles. Charley came down with such a case of dysentery he couldn't dig toilet holes fast enough and had to go to the temporary hospital at the back of the march. This was an old school building filled with sick men. There were some wounded soldiers as well, but he quickly learned that four men died of dysentery and disease for every man who died of battle wounds and he decided not to stay.

The doctor, a kind officer named Hand, gave him a shot of whiskey and some powder to mix in water and he went back to his company and arrived there in the late afternoon as the men were preparing for action.

"You're just in time," a private named Nelson told him. "We're going up to that line of trees and kick the Rebs out."

Charley studied the trees that lay two hundred yards off. Nelson was a new man—had come in with a batch of replacements from Minnesota that had caught up to them in the camp around Washington. Charley looked at him, saw the innocence, and felt his own age. Not in years. He was only sixteen. But in meadows. He was old in the art of crossing meadows. He wanted to tell Nelson about it, about what would be waiting when they went up to that line of trees to "kick the Rebs out." He opened his mouth, started to say something, then stopped. There was too much, a world too much to say. You couldn't say it. You had to live it. You had to see it.

"You don't know nothing," he told Nelson. "You don't know as much as a slick-eared calf."

Nelson stopped working on his rifle. "Well, ain't you one to take on airs? I guess I know enough—I know all I'll need."

Charley began to say more but instead just shook his head and walked away, looking for some cartridges to fill his box.

It started the same way again, this third time. The officers dismounted and moved to the front with their sabers, the sergeants just to their rear screaming at the men.

"All right! Form on me! Line-of-battle here!"

Charley stepped forward with the rest. He did not think of fear, did not think of what would happen, what he *knew* would happen. He stepped forward in line, checked the cap on his rifle and fixed his bayonet, and when they ordered, he started walking across the field with the rest of the men.

"Lord . . ."

There was no sound except for the clink of metal against metal on their shoulder straps, and Charley heard Nelson's voice whispering next to him.

"Lord, there they are, right there. See them?"

Charley said nothing but Nelson was right. He too could see the Rebel soldiers. This time they were not behind earthworks but were forming in ranks in front of the trees, just as the Union soldiers had done.

"They're going to come at us," Nelson said. "They're forming to attack us."

And even as he said it the Rebel soldiers began to scream and run forward at them. There was still no firing—the distance was too great—but the scream could easily be heard. It was the first time Charley was to hear the Rebel yell and for a moment it frightened him, but everything had to be compared and he thought of the fright of the first day, first battle, and the yell was nothing.

This was not a line of earthworks, with shells coming from cannons. This was not a hidden line of fire and death.

These were men, only men, no matter the yelling, and as the Rebels came running toward them the Union officers stopped the marching soldiers.

"Present arms!"

Charley raised his rifle.

"Ready—aim low, aim at their legs—*fire!*"

The men fired as one and the front rank of advancing Rebels went down.

"Reload and fire at will!"

Charley bit a cartridge without taking his eyes off the Rebels. They were still coming, but slower, the charge broken by the first volley, and he reloaded and fired four times, each time aiming low, and was reloading the fifth time when an officer to his front raised his saber.

"At them, men!" he screamed. "Give them steel!"

He started running at the confused Confederate line, and the Union soldiers followed, bayonets extended to the front.

Where's your yell now? Charley thought, and then realized that he was screaming it. "Where's your damn yell now?"

The Confederates started to hold, tried to stand. They fired once at the charging Union soldiers and out of the corner of his eye Charley saw men fall. But five smashing volleys of accurate fire had demoralized the Rebels, cut their numbers at least in half, and when they saw the blue line coming at them through the powder smoke, saw the glint of the bayonets, it was more than they could stand and they turned and ran.

"Look—they're showing tail," a man next to Charley yelled as they ran, and Charley glanced at him, surprised. Nelson had been there. Cocky Nelson. He was nowhere to be seen and Charley hadn't seen him get hit, hadn't seen him fall. Charley ran on.

Some men slowed, satisfied that they'd won the fight, but Charley couldn't stop running and soon found himself in front of the line. He would have been shocked to see himself. His lips were drawn back showing his teeth, and his face was contorted by a savage rage.

He wanted to kill them. He wanted to catch them and run his bayonet through them and kill them. All of them. Stick and jab and shoot them and murder them and kill them all, each and every Rebel's son of them. Not one would be able to get up. Not one. Kill them all.

Before they could kill *him.*

He was out of himself, beside himself, an animal, and it is difficult to say how far he would have gone; certainly he would have caught up with them and since he was nearly alone, and would have been alone when he did so, he would have been killed. But one of the sergeants stuck the butt of his rifle between Charley's ankles and brought him down.

"Better hold up there, gamecock—you can't take the whole Rebel army. Besides, they don't want any more of you. Let them go."

Charley sat on the ground, still snarling, watching the retreating Rebels. "We have to kill them. . . ."

"You'll get another chance," the sergeant

said, smiling. "Now re-form and let's get a line fixed again." He turned away and yelled at the other men. "On me—line-of-battle! Form line-of-battle!"

Charley got up and reloaded his rifle. The Rebels had gotten back into the trees and were firing, sniping at the Union lines, but the bullets all went high.

"Withdraw!" the sergeant yelled. "In formation, in good order, withdraw!"

They moved back across the field and had gone perhaps forty paces when Charley saw Nelson.

He was sitting on the ground, one hand holding his stomach. Charley broke rank and went to kneel beside him.

"Where are you hit?" He already knew the answer. Blood and other matter slid through Nelson's fingers onto the ground.

"Belly," Nelson said. "I got me a belly wound. Wouldn't you know it? First fight and I get me a belly wound." He gasped the words. The pain was already making it hard for him to breathe and Charley knew the real pain hadn't truly started yet.

"You'll be fine," Charley said. "The ambulance will come here and get you and you'll be back in Minnesota in no time—"

"Don't," Nelson said through his teeth. "Don't lie. They don't pick up men with belly wounds and you know it. They'll give me some water and leave me to die."

Charley didn't say anything but knew it was true. Stomach wounds were fatal. The surgeons could do nothing. The ambulance drivers would go through the wounded—when and if they got to the field—and jerk shirts up checking for stomach wounds. Those soldiers would be left. The surgeons were too busy with amputations and treatable injuries to spend time on those with stomach wounds.

It was an agonizingly slow death—it might

take two days—and the pain left men screaming until they were too hoarse to make another
sound.

"I don't want to die like this," Nelson said.
"Just laying here waiting for it . . ."

Charley didn't say anything because there
was nothing to say.

"Load my rifle, will you, Charley? I fired it
just as I was hit. Load it for me just in case the
Rebs come back, will you?"

Charley hesitated, then nodded and picked
up Nelson's rifle, tore a cartridge off with his
teeth, poured the powder down the bore and
settled the bullet on the powder.

"Don't forget the cap, Charley. Seat the cap
good."

Charley pinched a cap and set it on the nipple, pushing it down tightly with his thumb. He
put the hammer on half cock.

"Just put the rifle next to me, with the butt
down by my foot. Yes, like that. Now cock the

hammer, will you? Thank you. That's right kind of you, Charley. Just one more thing. I can't reach down to my foot and there's a powerful itch on my right foot. Would you take my shoe off before you go so I can scratch it?"

Charley unlaced the shoe and pulled it off. The foot was white, so white it looked like marble, as if it wasn't alive. Well, he thought, soon enough.

"I got me a letter back in my haversack where we put them down before we formed up," Nelson said. "Would you see that it gets mailed back to my folks in Deerwood? And tell them, if you see them, that I died with my face to the enemy, will you?"

Charley nodded and was surprised to find that he was crying. He did not think he could cry any longer but the tears were sliding down his cheeks. "Do you have water?"

Nelson nodded.

"Just take small sips," Charley said. "They say to just take small sips."

"Thank you for this—after I snotted back at you that way."

"That was nothing."

"Thank you anyway."

"It's nothing." Charley took a breath. The sergeant was coming back across the meadow toward him. One of the rules, he knew, was that you didn't stop for the wounded. When a man went down he was alone, even if he was your brother. "You want me to stay with you?"

Nelson shook his head. "They might be ready for another attack."

Charley stood and waved the sergeant back. "Well, then . . ."

"Yes—you'd better go."

Charley nodded but his feet didn't want to move. He had to force them, think about them moving, and with that he walked slowly. It was strange, he thought, the crying. I don't even rightly know him—still don't know his first name—and here I am crying. With all the men I've seen drop and I don't even know him and—

The sound of the shot stopped him. He stood for a moment, the tears working down his face, stood for a long moment and then started walking again. He did not look back.

Second battle.

CHAPTER SEVEN

TOWN LIFE

They went into camp again and this time they sat for three months. They were there so long they thought of the camp as a town and gave the paths between the tents street names based on Minnesota towns. Soon signs were stuck on poles: Winona Avenue, Taylor Falls Street . . .

It went from summer into fall and they cut trees and made log shanties and drilled in the rain and then snow, but spent most of their time in the log huts plugging leaks, keeping out cold wind and trying to get their clothes dry. They were rarely successful.

Disease spread through the camp like fire as the weather worsened, and with the disease came the rumors.

It was said that McClellan was afraid to fight. Almost all the men—including Charley—loved the new commander and felt that he was only trying to be easy on the men by avoiding a winter campaign. But the rumors said that Lincoln—most of the men also loved the president and called him Old Rail Splitter—was very dissatisfied with McClellan's "lack of bite" and wanted some attack made on the Rebels, somewhere, at some time soon.

This did not translate into action and the men sat another month, getting sicker and sicker, both physically and in their spirits.

Rumor said that a whole regiment from New York had deserted and gone home. It turned out not to be true—four men had deserted from a New York regiment and had been caught and tried and shot by firing squads— but it showed the lack of morale.

Another rumor said that a young general named Grant out west in Tennessee had fetched the Rebels such a hit that he'd whipped their western army and that Grant was a drunk and that Lincoln had said, "Find out what kind of whiskey he's drinking and send a case to *all* the generals." This proved to be the truth, but none of it really mattered to Charley.

Like most of the men, he worked at taking care of himself. It kept him busy. The camp was worse than a pigsty. Men from the country—most of the Minnesota volunteers—knew of country living. They dug holes for latrines, kept their areas cleaner than others and worked at getting good shelter. Men from cities—New Yorkers were the worst—had little concept of living with the land and no idea how to take care of themselves. They left sewage in the open, didn't drain the slops from their shelters and consequently were virtually destroyed by disease. Some New York companies lost more than half their men to dysentery, typhus, measles and diarrhea, which soon spread to other units.

It seemed somebody was always either getting sick, was sick, or was getting over something.

Charley and the rest were kept moving just working at repairing the shelter, keeping it clean and cooking. The food was simple and for the most part bad: beans, always beans, salt pork and coffee. Soon a bakery with wood-fired ovens was going and bread was doled out to the men. The plan was to give each man a pound of bread a day but it rarely worked out that well. The sutlers kept plying their trade and brought cakes and pies and cookies to the men, but the prices went up—fifty cents for a

cake that tasted as if it was made of wood—
and most of the men only bought from the sutlers in dire emergency. Charley once relented
and bought an apple pie but when he sat down
to eat it there were only three small slices of
apple in it and nearly no sugar.

If they had the ingredients housewives on
nearby farms cooked and sold meals to the
men, but getting food this way was chancy, to
say the least. There were over ninety thousand
men in the camp and perhaps twenty farms
where food might be available. To feed all the
men three meals a day, the farm wives would
have had to make thirteen to fifteen thousand
meals a day each. Besides, the officers seemed
to get most of this good food.

Officers were initially the only ones allowed
whiskey as well. Charley didn't drink but like
everybody else thought it unfair in the extreme
that only officers were considered able to han-
dle it. There was a small mutiny among some

of the units and soon whiskey was made available to all troops, although the enlisted men were to be issued it by the sutlers—a shot a day "to ward off the ague, chill and fever of winter camp"—and were supposed to drink it right where it was issued.

There was very little that was fair about the whole situation, at least from Charley's viewpoint, and it quickly became obvious to him that it was every man for himself.

He became adept at camp survival. He pulled his own weight, took his turn gathering food and wood, and cleaning, and cooking, but he made a private world for himself where he kept his thoughts and knowledge. He worked constantly on his equipment, shining the leather, changing his cartridges if they became damp or seemed even a bit moist, and most of all tending to his feet and his rifle.

"Charley, you're going to wear that rifle out," a man named Campbell told him one night while they sat by the trench stove. They had learned how to dig a trench a foot wide and a foot deep along the floor of their shelter, then out under a wall and into the open. The trench was covered with flat rocks and a barrel placed over the opening outside to make a passable chimney. When the men built a fire in the trench inside the log hut, the rocks would become hot and heat the whole shelter.

Charley looked up at Campbell, then back to his rifle. He had forgotten none of what had happened. He knew it would come again. It had to come again because they were here. You did not have an army without a battle. It was what the generals wanted, what they needed: a battle to use their armies. On both sides it was all up to the generals, the officers. If it was left up to the men who did the killing and dying there would be no war.

Death would still come.

"I'll be needing this rifle." He spoke down, as if talking to the weapon. He did not like to look at people as much as he once did. He did not like to learn about them. It was better if he didn't know them, become too friendly with them. They died so fast.

"*Pshaw!* We'll be in this camp all winter. They ain't going to fight when it's cold."

Charley said nothing but he remembered a night on guard duty. Down along the river he was put on picket duty, making sure there would be a warning if the Rebs on the other side of the river decided to attack. That night he was hunkered down behind an oak to get out of the wind—it was so cold he was reminded of Minnesota—and he heard a voice come from across the river, low and in a soft drawl.

"Hey, Union, can you hear me?"

Charley didn't answer.

"Blue belly, are you deaf?"

Oh well, Charley thought, why not talk to them? "What do you want?"

"Just to talk, maybe do a little trading."

"Trade bullets," Charley said. "That's all you want."

"Naw—it's too cold to fight. I've got me some good cut tobacco over here. You got any coffee? We're down to burned oats for coffee of a mornin'."

As it happened Charley had an extra half pound of coffee beans he'd been issued that afternoon. For months they hadn't had coffee at all and had been using burned oats themselves for a hot morning drink, but when ration came, as usual the army would get it wrong and issue triple rations. Now there was a glut of coffee.

Charley didn't use tobacco but he knew men who did, and Southern tobacco was much better than the foreign tobacco available to the Union army now that the South had seceded. He could trade the tobacco for bread, pies and leather to fix his shoes.

"How we going to trade?" Charley called back.

"I got me a plank. I'll throw a line over to your side on a rock and you pull the plank across with the tobacco and I'll pull it back with the coffee. Don't you shoot me when I stand up."

"I won't."

There was a half-moon and Charley peeked around the oak and watched as a slight figure stood up across the river. He was dressed poorly, his feet wrapped in what looked like sacks and his coat tattered and worn. Even in the moonlight he could see that the boy's face was dirty. He thought, I probably look the same. But the Reb looked even younger than Charley.

"Mind the stone," the boy called, and threw a rock with a string tied to it. The river was forty feet wide and the string snarled on the first toss and he had to retrieve it and toss it twice more before the rock made it. Charley moved from behind the oak and picked up the string. He kept low—couldn't help it—but in a few minutes he had pulled the board across the river and found the tobacco wrapped in a cloth. He wrapped his coffee beans and put the package on the plank.

"All right—pull it back," he called, and the piece of wood made its way back across the water. Charley watched it until it reached the other bank and then he moved behind the oak, squatted down out of sight and tucked the tobacco inside his coat.

"Hey, blue belly—you still there?"

"I'm here."

"This coffee looks good. Can you get more?"

"Some."

"Let's trade again tomorrow night. I can get all the tobacco you need."

"All right."

There was another silence, then: "Where you from, Union?"

"Minnesota."

"Where's that?"

How could he not know where Minnesota was? "Up north—north of Iowa."

"Oh. I'm from Alabama. You a farmer?"

"I worked on farms."

"Me too. What do you grow?"

"Potatoes, corn, squash, wheat and oats and barley."

"Same as us except we have greens and 'baccy and some rice in the bottoms. This is right stupid, ain't it?"

"What?"

"Here we be, both farmers, talking and trading goods and tomorrow or the next day we got to shoot at each other."

I hope, Charley thought, you don't hit me.

"Ain't it stupid?" the boy asked.

"Yes."

"I've got to go now. My trick is near up. I'll yell for you tomorrow night."

And that was it. There was no further talk or

trading because an officer had heard Charley and jumped him about speaking to the enemy, and the same must have happened to the Reb because the next night Charley leaned against the oak and somebody fired from the other side of the river and drew splinters off the tree four feet over his head.

The truce was over.

CHAPTER EIGHT

WINTER

He felt alone now. Always alone. He existed in a world that he believed—no, *knew*—would end for him soon. In the middle of the unit, drilling, eating, listening to the officers with men sitting packed all around him, he was alone.

Charley was one of the men detailed to provide beef for the sick men in the hospital—another school building the army had temporarily commandeered—but there were no cattle available.

"Look to the Rebel horses," the doctor said. "The men have to have meat."

There had been a brush with the Confederate cavalry along the river. A Rebel unit had made a discovery raid early one morning and had the bad luck to run into a full company of Union soldiers with loaded rifles already arranged in firing order for a defensive drill. The outcome had resulted in many empty Rebel saddles and eleven captured horses.

Normally the horses would be used to pull artillery—the death rate for horses in combat was worse than that for men because they were a much bigger target.

But in this case it was decided to kill the horses to get meat for the sick men, and Charley and three other soldiers were ordered to slaughter them.

It did not bother Charley to kill beef or pigs or poultry but having to shoot each horse in the head and cut its throat and gut it and skin it put him on the edge of mutiny. He had been raised with workhorses and had come to love them. Killing the horses—watching them drop as they were shot in the head—made him almost physically ill.

It was a miserable day. They lied to the sick men and told them it was beef but those men knew. Horse fat is yellow, yellow as butter, and beef fat is white, and the men knew the meat was from horses. They ate it anyway, and were grateful, but the whole day struck a sour note that added to Charley's general gloom. At four the next morning, when they were called out into formation to march south, he was in a foul mood.

They had had no warning of the impending movement, and rumors flew: There was a big battle coming; there had been a big battle and they were going to march all the way to Richmond; the South had lost the war; the South had *won* the war.

Charley stomped around at first, still angry over slaughtering the horses. But it was a fine morning, so cold that the muddy roads were frozen and made for easy walking, and the troops made good time.

They walked all day—Charley thought it must have been close to twenty miles. After a while the men were too tired and winded to talk and there was silence. At just after three in the afternoon Charley heard the sounds of artillery booming about two miles off.

He had a practiced ear now for the tools of combat and knew from the frequency of fire— a constant thunder—that there were a lot of guns, which meant a lot of targets. As his unit drew closer he heard the rattling-ripping sound of thousands of rifles being fired. Soon, he knew, he would be involved in the fighting.

He checked his cartridge box as he walked, making sure his rifle was loaded and capped, and felt the fear building. Always the fear.

The men marched down a country lane in

the late afternoon. At any other time it would have been a beautiful place. Trees lined the roadway and though their leaves were gone the bare branches bent over the road, creating a cover. The sun shone through and dappled the road in light but Charley saw none of it.

The sounds were louder now, much louder, and the chattering of the rifles was continuous.

Half a mile, he thought—it's just half a mile to the fighting. He listened expertly while they marched. The lane ended a quarter mile ahead in a T. Some of the firing was off to the right, but most was to the left. They would probably be told to move left—into the worst of the firing.

For a change Charley was wrong. At the end of the T they were stopped.

"Throw down your packs and bedrolls. Carry only your rifle, cartridges, bayonet and canteens. Form line-of-battle to the right! To the right!" sergeants yelled.

The officers on horses dismounted and with

the sergeants directed the men down the road until they were stretched a quarter mile, then across a rail fence into a field of grain stubble.

Always a field, Charley thought—there's always fear and always a meadow.

Once out in the open he could see more of the battle. In front of him, for the moment, there were no soldiers, Rebel or Union, just a field that stretched away a quarter mile to a line of trees. There was no foliage in the trees but even as bare as they were he could see no Rebel troops or artillery to their front.

Off to their left, well away—close to a mile—an absolute inferno raged. Artillery from both sides covered the battlefield with smoke, and the din of cannon and rifle fire was constant and deafening. Whenever the smoke cleared in small gusts of breeze he could see men dropping by the hundreds, broken and crumpled and falling.

Nothing, Charley thought as he watched the

fight, absolutely nothing could live through that, and he was grateful that it was happening to others and not him.

"There they are!" somebody near him cried. "In the trees . . ."

Charley squinted and saw them. Not infantry this time. But assembling back in the trees were troops of cavalry, the horses jostling each other and kicking as they were pulled alongside each other.

"They're going to come at us! They're sending horse against us!" somebody yelled.

"Ready on line!" An officer in front of them walked back and forth with a saber. "Do not fire until directed and then fire at will. On my command the first time! Front ranks kneel."

Charley was in the second rank and he stood while the front rank kneeled. The horses moved out of the trees, walking forward in a line.

Close on a hundred of them, Charley

thought, watching. They're a hundred and they're going to try to ride over us. He saw the glint of sun on cavalry sabers and carbines. They were still three hundred yards distant but he could see the shine of horses' hair and the splash of light off bridle hardware and chest straps. The horses began to walk faster, and then trot, the men holding them in good line.

"Present arms!" officers and sergeants called, and men raised their rifles, cocking the hammers.

"Wait for it . . . wait for it. Not yet, boys, not yet." A sergeant in front moved back into the ranks to get out of the line of fire. "Aim for the horses. When you get the command, aim low—hit the horses to break the men."

More meat for the sick, Charley thought, and felt bad for having to kill the horses. He didn't fret the men at all. They were going to kill him and he didn't mind killing them first. But he hated shooting the horses.

They started to canter. Two hundred yards now. A hundred and fifty.

"Ready!"

One hundred yards. The Rebel troopers were screaming that chuttering, high-pitched Rebel yell, and the horses were full out, eating the distance.

Fifty yards. I could hit them with a chucked corncob, Charley thought. Spit flying out of the horses' mouths, hooves rumbling against the frozen ground; we'll never stop them, Charley thought, no way in Hades can we stop them.

"Fire!"

At no more than thirty yards, over six hundred men fired in a volley at a hundred charging horses. The result was devastating.

Charley held high and took a trooper full in the chest, but most of the other men held on the horses and not one animal came through unhit. In a great cloud they went down, somersaulting, rolling over the troopers on their backs, breaking themselves and the men; and the screams—the screams of the wounded horses hit by soft, large-caliber expanding bullets, horses with heads blown open, horses with jaws shot away, horses with eyes shot out or with intestines tangling in their hooves, horses torn and dying—screamed louder than a thousand, louder than a million men.

"Reload and fire at will!"

Charley automatically loaded, raised and fired, but there were few targets. Those horses back on their feet were quickly shot down and any man who stood was hit ten, twenty times.

"Cease fire!"

Silence except for the screaming horses and the groaning of wounded men. Charley reloaded, capped his rifle and kneeled, resting. He was thirsty and took a sip from his canteen. He did not look at the horses stumbling and kicking and falling.

Was that it? he wondered—just the one

charge? It was nearly dark now—a soft dusk—
and he looked to the rear to see where they
might camp for the night and get fires going
for coffee and heat. He loved coffee, though it
tore his guts and gave him a constant stomach-
ache, and he thought of going to the shattered
Confederate charge to see if they had any
sugar in their saddlebags. There was good
sugar in the South and he might find some for
his coffee. He salivated, thinking of coffee with
sugar in it.

"On the left! Form line-of-battle and wheel
left!"

He turned and his heart nearly stopped.
Coming from their left oblique, walking
toward them in the gathering twilight, seemed
to be the whole Rebel army.

Two thousand, Charley thought. Maybe
three thousand of them. Marching straight at
Charley in a head-on attack.

"Range four hundred!" the sergeants called.

"Set sights for four hundred. Fire when ready."

Charley thought it more like three hundred yards but he flipped up the rear sight for four hundred and raised and fired. He didn't hear his rifle because everybody around him fired at the same time.

Some of the Rebels fell. Not many, not nearly enough. Charley reloaded and fired, then again and again, and each time the Union soldiers fired more of the Rebels fell—jerking backward and down, spinning forward, sitting back with the shock of being hit.

The Rebels had not fired yet but had started to trot. They were down to two hundred and fifty yards and Charley and the men around him kept up a steady rate of fire. Charley fired fifteen rounds and hit perhaps seven or eight Rebels, but most of the men shot high—a common failing when firing on advancing infantry.

They were only seventy-five yards away now.

It was nearly dark and the flash from the rifles momentarily blinded Charley.

At fifty yards the Rebels fired and at least fifteen hundred bullets tore into the Union line. Men went down in droves—twenty around Charley alone. His own clothing was hit four times, the brim on his cap sliced off, wood knocked off the stock of his rifle and one of his shoe heels creased.

"Fix bayonets!"

It was to be steel, Charley saw. The men from Minnesota could have run but didn't; they held their ground, and Charley held with them. With his bayonet locked onto his muzzle, he loaded one last time just as the Rebels hit the Union line.

Oh, he thought, this is nasty work. This is right *nasty* work. It was nearly dark and hard to tell uniforms apart in the bad light and the smoke from firing, and Charley did not know where to turn, where to fight. The decision wasn't his. In the murk a man suddenly appeared, his bayoneted rifle aimed at Charley's chest. Charley parried with his own rifle and took the Rebel soldier just below the breastbone with his bayonet. The man had been running so hard he ran himself onto the bayonet before falling off to the side, dying as he fell, his lungs and heart torn. Charley's bayonet was stuck and he had to put his foot on the man's chest to jerk it loose.

After that there was no order, no sense, no plan. Charley became a madman. He attacked anything and everything that came into his range—slashing, clubbing, hammering, jabbing, cutting—and always screaming, screaming in fear, in anger and finally in a kind of rabid, insane joy, the joy of battle, the joy of winning, the joy of killing to live.

And at last there was nothing around to hit, to fight, to kill. He stood with the rifle hanging at his side, his bayonet bent at the tip, the stock shattered, his arms weak, his legs soft, his chest heaving as he sucked air, his throat rasping.

"They've run," somebody said. "They've took foot."

"You're hit." A corporal stood in front of Charley.

"No. I'm all right."

"You're hit there, in the shoulder."

Charley looked down. He was covered in blood, his arm and chest and pants wet with it. "Oh . . ."

"The surgeon's tent is back there a half mile, in those trees. Can you walk it?"

"I think so."

"Go it, then. Get patched. We'll see you later."

Charley walked in a kind of daze, dragging his broken rifle by the sling. With the dark the temperature had plummeted but he didn't feel the cold. He didn't feel anything.

He saw the lanterns of the surgeon and the ambulance drivers and walked toward them. Somebody in a bloody apron stopped him and held a lantern up, lighting his face with a yellow glow.

"Where are you hit?"

"I don't know. They sent me back. I think it's my shoulder but it don't seem to hurt."

"Over there. Sit with that group by the tent and we'll get to you when we can." The man turned back to the tent with no sides where a doctor working by lantern light was sawing a leg off a soldier. Near the tent was a pile of arms and legs that stood four feet high and ten or twelve feet long.

Ambulance wagons kept coming with more men, and Charley moved to an area where fifteen or twenty men lay on the ground waiting for attention. Off to the other side of the tent there was another group of two or three hundred men. They were not moving and Charley realized they were dead.

He sat and waited for the pain to come. Once when he was a boy he'd struck his foot with an ax. The blade had cut a three-inch gash between two of his toes and he'd walked to town to get it sewed up. It hadn't hurt for the entire walk, hadn't hurt until the doctor had stitched it up and he'd walked home. Then it had kept him up all night.

He thought it would be the same here but the pain didn't come. He tried to sip some water from his canteen but it had frozen into slush and wouldn't drain through the neck of the bottle, so he lay back on the ground. Men around him moaned and some died waiting to be taken under the tent.

Presently—it could have been an hour, a day, a week, for Charley no longer thought in terms of time, no longer really thought at all—the man with the bloody apron came back to him.

"Shuck your coat—let's see how bad you're hurt."

Charley unbuttoned his greatcoat, then his uniform jacket and his flannel shirt.

"Let's see . . ." The attendant held the lantern up, pulled the shirt away and looked down the front and back. "Hell, boy, you ain't hit."

"I'm not?"

"Not a scratch. That's other men's blood all over you."

"Oh."

"You can go back."

"Not yet." A doctor came out of the tent. "I need help here. The wind is making up and the cold is freezing my hands. I need some kind of windbreak—see if the two of you can't fix something up."

"With what?" The attendant looked around. "There's nothing here."

The doctor looked around, then back, then at the bodies. "Use *them.*"

"The dead?"

"They won't feel it. You"—he pointed a

bloody hand at Charley—"give him help there. Pile them up to stop the wind from the side of the tent."

And so they did. Each taking an end, they moved the bodies, stacking them like bricks and angling them at the corners so they would not tip over, until they had a stout frozen wall five feet high and thirty feet long to stop the wind.

When it was done Charley lay on the ground in the lee of the dead men's wall, just to get out of the wind for a minute and get warm, and slept there for five hours, sheltered by the dead.

Third battle.

CHAPTER NINE

—◆—

GETTYSBURG

It was in many respects exactly the same and yet completely different.

He had been in more skirmishes and he had killed more men. He had had men die next to him. But he had not been in another major battle.

Now he was at Gettysburg, Pennsylvania, on top of a gradually sloping hill, looking down at what seemed to be the entire Southern army assembling to attack.

What was the same was the meadow. There

was always a forest and always a meadow. In this case the forest where the Rebels were assembling was over a mile away and well below the Union army. In between was a large meadow a mile or more wide. The Rebels would have to leave the trees and walk, under constant fire from artillery, across the meadow and up the incline to the fences and rock walls where the Union soldiers waited.

What was different about this battle was that Charley was above the Rebs, in a sheltered position, with all the guns in the world behind him.

It was a warm day and he sipped some water from his canteen and checked his rifle. He had taken a new one from a dead man after his own had been destroyed. This rifle had a tendency to foul its nipple, so he carried a small needle stuck in his shirt to clean the hole out if it plugged. He did so now and put a fresh cap on the nipple, then tightened his shoelaces in case he had to run. That was always in his mind—either run at them or run away. He did not want to stumble.

He peeked through the rock wall again and saw the Confederate artillery wheeling their cannon into place. The Rebs would try to prepare the hill with artillery before their charge, and as Charley looked the first batteries began firing. Soon they were all hammering away. It was the worst barrage Charley had undergone. Shells burst overhead and killed men and horses and destroyed some Union artillery and rear positions.

But it could have been far worse. The line of Union troops waiting to take the Confederate attack were at the brow of the hill, which dropped away to their rear as well. The Rebel artillery was massed and firing heavily, but rounds aimed at the top of the hill that went even slightly high just passed over and exploded down the back side.

Casualties were not as heavy as all the noise and smoke indicated. When shooting tapered off and the Rebels started moving their massed troops across the meadow and up the hill, the Union artillery wheeled into position and tore into them with exploding rounds: chain and grapeshot. The Confederates had to march through a storm of fire and Charley lay and watched them and nearly felt sorry for them.

They were so brave, he thought—or foolish. They kept coming, even when thousands of them were down and dying. The cannon ripped them to pieces, wiping them out before they were even within rifle range, slaughtering them like sheep as they marched in even rows. Sometimes whole rows were dropped where they stood, so the dead lay in orderly lines. And still they came on.

At first it all seemed so distant, as if it was a staged tableau. Men marched, then they spun and fell, exploding red bursts into the air.

But as they came closer and Charley could see what the artillery was doing to them—tearing, gutting, blowing apart—he could not believe that anyone would continue, *could* continue against the fire.

Yet they came on and on, close enough now so those not hit could return fire, and Charley could hear their bullets hitting the rocks in front of him and he thought, so this is what it's like to be safe, to fight from a good position.

"All right—up, men." The sergeants roused them. "Ready to fire! Shoot low, shoot low—take their legs out. Present, aim, fire!"

Charley raised, aimed and fired, all in less than two seconds. He did not know if he hit, did not care. He reloaded behind the wall, rose, aimed, fired, and thought, this is the way it should be done. The bullets over his head sounded like a storm but they were all high, and he kept reloading and firing as the remaining Rebs screamed and started to run at the wall.

"Up, men! Bayonets! Take them."

Charley did not think any of the Rebels would reach the line but they came on. Torn and bleeding and many in rags, they yelled and came with bayonets, and for a moment it seemed they would carry it, win the hill, win the battle against impossible odds.

But a colonel saw the danger and ordered the only unit still in relative shelter—the First Minnesota Volunteers—to make a counter-charge.

They rose and went as one man, Charley among them. Screaming their own yells, they tore down the hill at the Rebel unit storming up the hill, and the two bodies of men collided in a smash of steel and powder, standing toe-to-toe, hacking and shooting at each other, neither giving, climbing over the bodies of friends to hit enemies, Charley in the middle jabbing and screaming until he was hit, and hit again, spun and knocked down, and he saw the red veil come down over his eyes and knew that at last he was right, at last he was done, at last he was dead.

CHAPTER TEN

JUNE 1867

He could remember all the sweet things when it had started; waving pretty girls, Southern summer mornings, cheering children, dew on a leaf . . .

Even when all his thoughts came on to being gray and raining and the parades were done and the dances were done and the killing—he thought of it as butchery more than killing—was at last done, he could remember all the pretty things.

He was twenty-one now, just getting to

where he should be studying on marriage and raising some young ones, finding some land to work and improve. But it wouldn't be that way for him. He was too old. Not old in years—in years he still hadn't started daily shaving or learned about women. But in other ways he was old, old from too much life, old from seeing too much, old from knowing too much. He was tired and broken, walking with a cane and passing blood, and he knew it wouldn't be long for him. In some ways it made him sad and in some ways he was near glad of it. So many of the men he knew were there already, gone across, that he thought it might not be so bad to go see them, to get away from this constant pain and the sounds he couldn't stop hearing.

And so on this fine summer morning near Winona, Minnesota, he walked out along the river—limped was more like it—to have himself a picnic. He carried a feed sack with half a loaf of bread and some of Agile Peterson's cheese and a chunk of roast beef with fat in it and a jar of cold coffee. That was one thing that stuck with him. The army had taught him to like coffee, live on coffee, and he still drank it even though it knotted his guts.

Coffee and beans. He could still sit to a meal of coffee and beans and a little pork belly and not feel starved.

But not for a picnic. Not for this picnic. He wasn't sure in fact that he would eat. He'd come out on many such picnics before, not sure he would eat but just to sit on the river and wonder if it was time to go visit the others, and always he had eaten and had coffee and then walked—limped—back to his small house on the edge of town. He'd heard it called a shack. Charley's shack. But he thought of it as a house.

He found a place where a soft breeze kept the mosquitoes away, and the sun warmed the grass and dirt, and some rocks in the river made rippling sounds and he stopped and with great effort lowered himself into a sitting position. He sat with his legs straight out in front of him. It was an awkward position but his knees didn't want to bend and he couldn't lie back on the grass because it made him sick to lie down, so he sat, watching the river go by. Then he reached into the sack and took out the bread and cheese and set them on a small flat rock nearby. Then, as he removed the jar of coffee, his hands brushed the other thing in the sack and he took it out and put it on the rock near the bread and cheese.

It was a .36-caliber cap-and-ball revolver he'd taken off the body of a Confederate officer. Charley had known the man was dead because he'd just killed him with his bayonet, watching the steel slide in just over the belt buckle. He remembered taking the revolver.

Everybody wanted them, those Confederate

revolvers—back home they wanted them. "Pick me up a Confederate pistol," they'd say in letters. As if you'd just pick one up off the ground. As if they weren't being carried by Confederate soldiers who didn't want to give them away. As if you wouldn't have to kill men to get the revolvers . . .

He shook his head. That wasn't one of the things he liked to think about.

The revolver shone in the sun. It was clean and free of rust and corrosion, greased and capped and fully loaded, the walnut grips so shiny they looked deep and almost red.

It was a pretty thing, he thought. The revolver was as pretty as anything he'd seen, black and shining, and he held it for a moment, hefting it. He eased the hammer back until it clicked, looked at his finger on the trigger and knew that if he just touched it there, just a light touch, it would trip the hammer to slap the percussion cap and set off the powder and send the little .36-caliber ball speeding out of the barrel and into his . . .

He eased the hammer down with his thumb and laid the pistol back on the rock next to the cheese and then sat, listening to the ripple of the river, watching the water go by, thinking of all the pretty things.

AUTHOR'S NOTE

This is partly a work of fiction. Charley Goddard really existed. He enlisted in the First Minnesota Volunteers when he was fifteen, lying about his age, and fought through virtually the entire war.

I have had to take some minor liberties with timing because no one man could have been everywhere at once. Charley, for instance, did not fight at Bull Run, although that was about the only battle he missed. He did not fight because he was laid up with dysentery. But in all respects everything in this book happened, either to Charley or to men around him. Every event is factual, including the building of a wall of dead bodies to stop the wind. Charley really did receive wounds at Gettysburg. The destruction at Gettysburg was nearly biblical in its proportions; more men were killed there in just two hours than in all the previous American wars, the Revolution included, *combined*. When the battle at

Gettysburg was finished and they'd made their fateful charge, only forty-seven men were left standing of the thousand original soldiers of the First Minnesota Volunteers.

Charley was not one of them. He was hit severely, and though they patched him up as best they could and he managed to fight in later actions, his wounds did not heal properly, nor did his mental anguish. When the war was finished he went back and tried to hold jobs and couldn't, eventually running for county clerk on the basis of his war record. He was elected, but before he could serve, his wounds and the stress took him and he died in December 1868.

He was just twenty-three years old.

SELECTED SOURCES

Orrin Fruit Smith and Family papers, Minnesota Historical Society.

BOOKS

Catton, Bruce.

The American Heritage New History of the Civil War. New York: Viking, 1996.

Grant Moves South: 1861–1863. Boston: Little Brown, 1990.

Grant Takes Command: 1863–1865. Boston: Little Brown, 1990.

A Stillness at Appomattox (Army of the Potomac, Vol. 3). New York: Anchor Press, 1953.

Gettysburg: The Final Fury. New York: Doubleday, 1974.

Terrible Swift Sword. New York: Doubleday, 1962.

This Hallowed Ground: The Story of the Union Side of the Civil War. New York: Doubleday, 1962.

SELECTED SOURCES

Foote, Shelby.
    Civil War: A Narrative (Vol. 1, *Fort Sumter to Perryville,* and Vol. 3, *Red River to Appomattox*). New York: Vintage Press, 1986.

    Stars in Their Courses: The Gettysburg Campaign. New York: Modern Library (reprint edition), 1994.

Moe, Richard.
    The Last Full Measure: The Life and Death of the First Minnesota Volunteers. New York: Avon, 1994.

Nofi, Albert A.
    A Civil War Treasury: Being a Miscellany of Arms and Artillery, Facts and Figures, Legends and Lore, Muses and Minstrels, Personalities and People. New York: Da Capo Press, 1995.

Sears, Stephen W.
    George B. McClellan. New York: Ticknor and Fields, 1988.

Read the Latest Thrilling Brian Adventure

From Bestselling Author Gary Paulsen

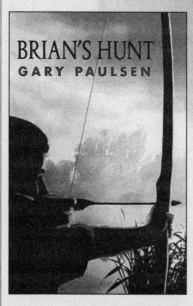

Brian is alone in the wilderness, or is he? When Brian finds a wounded dog, he senses danger. The dog is badly hurt, and as Brian cares for it, his instincts tell him to head north quickly to find out what attacked his new companion. Join Brian as he sets out on the hunt of a lifetime.

Read all the Brian Adventures

Available wherever books are sold.

WENDY
LAMB
BOOKS

www.randomhouse.com/teens

WELCOME TO THE WONDERFUL WORLD OF PUBERTY!

In this hilarious, honest, and ultimately optimistic book, Newbery Award-winning author Gary Paulsen puts his survival expertise to use against the most frightening wilderness of all—puberty!

Dare to explore: log on to
www.randomhouse.com/teens
for a complete list of books
by Gary Paulsen!

AVAILABLE WHEREVER BOOKS ARE SOLD.

Illustrations © Souther Salazar.

160